Shhh!

Be very,

very

quiet.

I just put **THE** most rascally dragon to sleep.

So turn the page very slowly,

and whatever you do. . .

2

. . . don't wake her up.

Oh no!

When the page turned, the breeze blew the door shut with a . . .

BANG!

Quick! Check to see if the dragon is still sleeping.

Phew!

Say *shhh* three times as you turn the page **very** carefully.

Shhh!
Shhh!
Shhh!

Oops!

The cooks in the castle's kitchen dropped some pots and pans.

CLINK!

CLANK!

CLASH!

Hey, Cooks! If you wake the dragon,
you take the dragon.

Let's see if she's still sleeping.

Stroke her scales gently along her back and . . .

. . . turn the page without making a sound.

HOW TO CATCH A MOUSE

FAIRY TALES

Oh no! Now the noisy knights next door are celebrating a birthday **very** loudly.

KNOCK! KNOCK! KNOCK! KNOCK!

PARTY This Way!

Knock on their door.

Sing happy birthday with them.

Happy birthday to you.

Happy birthday to you.

Happy birthday, dear friend.

Happy birthday to you!

Help
blow out
the candles.

Do a quick dance.

Wiggle   Jiggle

Giggle

Now politely ask them
to keep the noise down.

BOOM!

BANG!

BOOM!

BOOM-BANG!

I don't think they can hear you.
Try tapping on this drum.

That did the trick!

Ask them one more time to **PLEEEEASE** keep the noise down.

And we better check to see **if** the dragon is still sleeping.

Good!

She's still asleep.

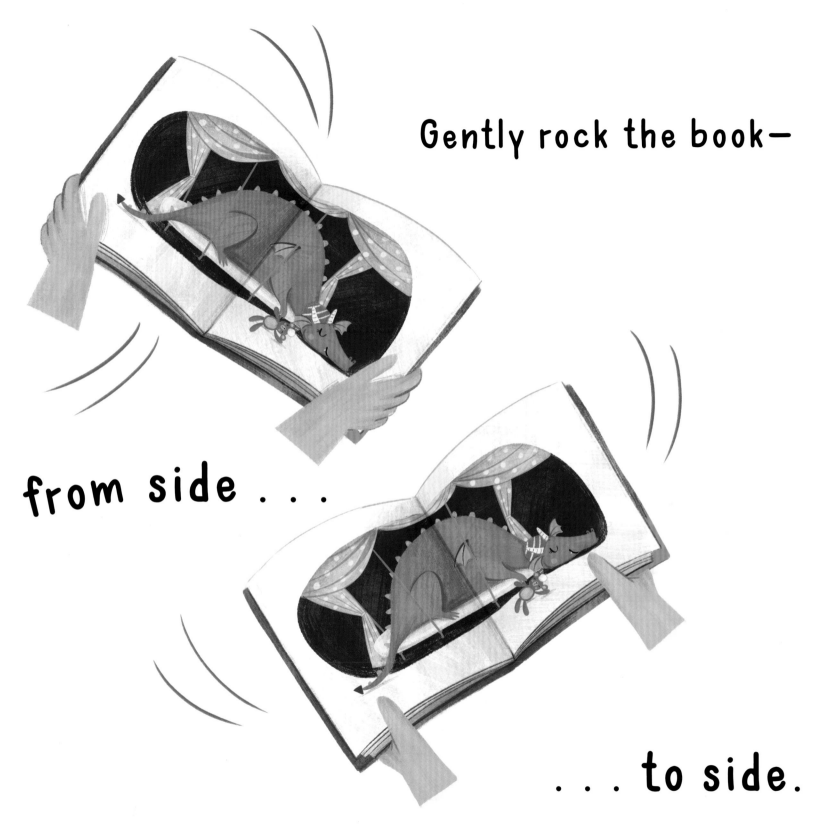

Gently rock the book—

from side . . .

. . . to side.

The entire kingdom is quiet now.
It's time for us to sleep, too.

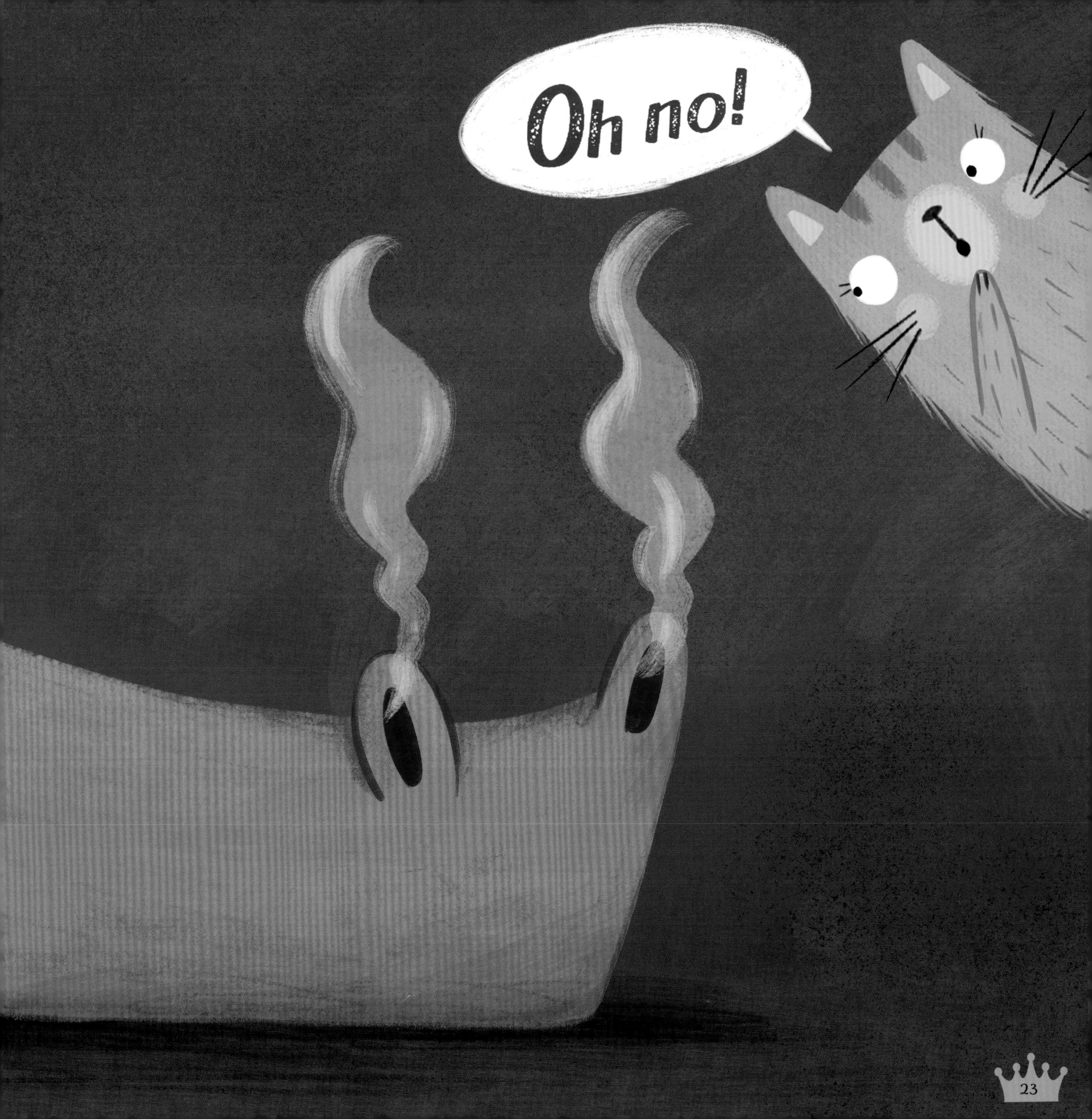
Oh no!

She woke up! What should we do?

Maybe we should stroke her scales?

She's still awake?

Hmmm...

Do you think dragons love lullabies?

Let's find out.

Sing along!

Dragon, dragon, close your eyes,

Time to listen to lullabies.

Tuck your tail and rest your scales,

Dream of fire-breathing dragon tales.

Dragon, dragon, time to sleep.

Lay so still . . .

don't make a peep.

Excellent! It's working. Lay your head on the pillow.

Tuck yourself in. Be very still, and say *shhh* three more times.

Now, close the book **very** gently.

Whatever you do . . .